The Day Leap Ate Olives

Written by Jim Marggraff
Illustrated by Yakovetic Productions

pins

hen

pop

fig

The hen was fat,
the table set.
Lil was still,
Tad's diaper, wet.

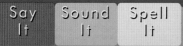

bun

cob

nut

JAM

GUM

Leap was scared.
He looked at Lil.
"Green olives! Yuck!"
He felt a chill.

pins

ham

pop

BIB

fish

yam

fig

Leap said, "I'll eat a yam and stew, corn on the cob, and catfish, too."

Say It   Sound It   Spell It

nuts

bun

hen

"But there's one thing I can not do, that's eat an olive, one or two!"

fish

 Dad dug six olives
off the heap.
Then set the tub
in front of Leap.

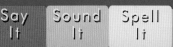

6

yam

olives

"Please take one olive from the heap," said Dad, as he looked straight at Leap.

corn

JAM

 "Dad?" Lil tried to set Leap free. "Can Leap pass that big tub to me?"

 Say It Sound It Spell It

clock

ham

six

 Leap got out
his olive jet,
put on the tub,
said, "Ready, set!"

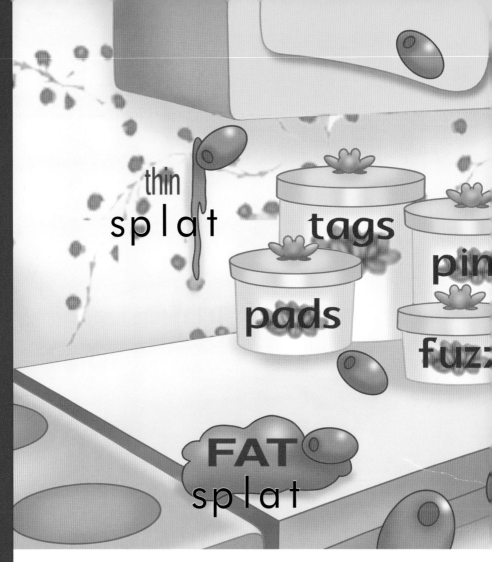

thin
splat

tags

pads

pin

fuzz

FAT
splat

 He set it up
and let it rip!
That olive jet
went zip, zap, ZIP!

Say It   Sound It   Spell It

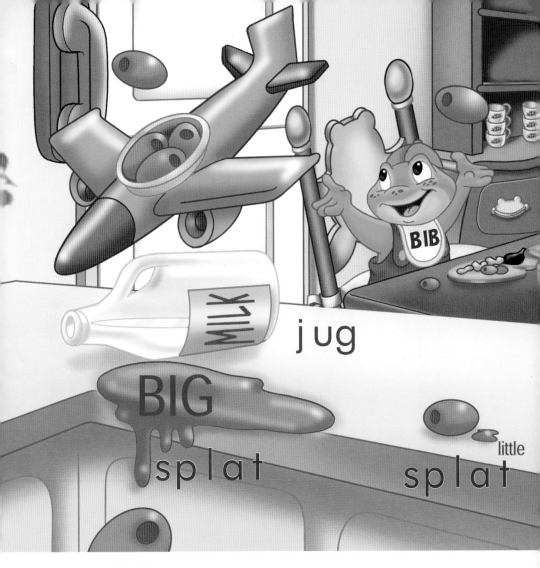

jug

BIG

splat

little
splat

The olives flew this way and that, each landing with a juicy SPLAT!

Mom

 "Dad," Leap said, "Oops. Too bad! That was the only tub we had!"

Say It   Sound It   Spell It

dish

cup

hen

JAM

"Leap," said Dad,
"Please have no fear.
We can fix that
problem. Here!"

rag
hot

mug

rug

 There, behind a
pot and pan,
Dad got a big
red olive can.

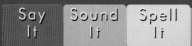

top

lid

cold

mitt

ON OFF

"Now tell me Leap,
and tell me true.
Just why do olives
bother you?"

puff

rust

duck

bug

 "Dad, in that tub, all I can see are eyeballs staring back at me!"

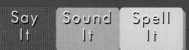

Say It   Sound It   Spell It

tub

nut

👂 "Oh, my!" said Mom.
"I might be sick!"
Tad squished an olive.
Lil said, "Ick!"

GO

 "Leap?" said Dad,
his voice quite kind.
"Shut your eyes,
and clear your mind."

STOP

 Say It   Sound It   Spell It

"Think of food you love to eat. Hot dogs, hopcorn, even sweets."

nuts

fig

cob

 Leap bit his lip and tried to grin, then shut his eyes and dug right in.

 Say It | Sound It | Spell It

He picked three olives, let them drop. In his mouth they plop, plop, PLOPPED!

top

logs box

Mom and Dad
smiled, so did Lil!
Tad went for
the olive hill!

22

Leap licked his lips and yummed a yum. He loved those olives, every one.

"That thing I
said I can not do?
Eating olives,
one or two?"

mop

block

top

"Well I was right!
For did you see?
I ate not one,
not two, but three!"

Say It Sound It Spell It